This Journal Belongs To:

FUTURE KING TOBIAS

Hardcover ISBN: 978-1-965966-00-6
Paperback ISBN: 978-1-965966-02-0
eBook ISBN: 978-1-965966-00-6
Cover & Layout by: Maggie Tortoledo Designs

DEAR PAPER,

I SAW NORA WRITING IN A BOOK AND IT
MADE ME WANT TO WRITE IN A BOOK.
BUT I DON'T KNOW WHAT TO WRITE OTHER
THAN

THEO SUCKS
NORA IS ANNOYING

I AM PERFECT

KING TOBIAS — AGE 7

DEAR PAPER,

MOTHER IS SAYING THAT WE SHOULD HAVE ANOTHER SIBLING SOON. THAT HER AND FATHER ARE TRYING? WHATEVER THAT MEANS.
SHE SHOULD BE HAPPY ABOUT ME.
AND MAYBE THEO. ONLY WHEN HE'S NOT ANNOYING.

NORA CAME AND I PUSHED HER. I SHOULD FEEL BAD, AUNT SYBIL YELLED AT ME. BUT I DON'T FEEL BAD.

SHE SHOULD LISTEN.

KING TOBIAS — AGE 7

DEAR PAPER,

NORA AND THEO RAN FROM ME TODAY.
THEY HAD A BASKET OF TREATS AND
RAN.

I WANTED TREATS TOO. WHY DID THE HIDE
FROM ME?

KING TOBIAS — AGE 8

DEAR PAPER,

TODAY IS NORA'S BIRTHDAY. SHE IS NOW 7.

SO I GUESS SHE'S NOT AS ANNOYING.

MOTHER'S BELLY IS BIG. TOO BIG TO GIVE

HUGS ANYMORE.

MOTHER KEEPS SAYING NORA IS A

MIRACLE AND SHE CAN'T WAIT FOR US TO

GET MARRIED. SHE ACTS AS IF I AM

OLDER THAN NINE. I AM A KID. I DON'T

WANT TO MARRY NORA YET.

I DON'T WANT TO MARRY HER AT ALL.

KING TOBIAS — AGE 9

DEAR PAPER,

i GOT MAD TODAY. i GET ANGRY REAL EASY NOW. BUT THEO AND NORA RAN AWAY AND HiD AGAIN. i DON'T LiKE THAT THEY ALWAYS HiDE FROM ME.

SO i PUSHED HER DOWN THE HiLL. THEO WAS HOLDING HER HAND. iM SUPPOSED TO HOLD HER HAND.

THAT'S WHAT MOTHER SAYS.

KiNG TOBiAS — AGE 9

DEAR PAPER,

AUNT SYBIL AND NORA WERE SUPPOSED
TO COME TODAY.

BUT THEY DIDN'T.

KING TOBIAS — AGE 9

MOTHER DIED TODAY.

SO DID THE BABY.

SHOULDN'T I FEEL SAD?

DEAR PAPER,

NORA IS MISSING AND AUNT SYBIL IS DEAD
TOO. FATHER IS ANGRY. HE HIT THEO
TODAY, I HID IN THE THRONE ROOM.
NO ONE KNOWS WHERE NORA IS.

MAYBE I CAN FIND HER?

KING TOBIAS — AGE 9

DEAR PAPER,

THEO IS UPSET. NORA HAS BEEN MISSING
FOR TWO WEEKS AND FATHER STOPPED
GETTING LETTERS FROM HER FATHER.

IS SHE DEAD TOO?

KING TOBIAS — AGE 9

DEAR PAPER,

SHE'S ALIVE.

SHOULDN'T i BE HAPPY ABOUT THAT?

KING TOBIAS — AGE 9

DEAR PAPER,

WE AREN'T ALLOWED TO SEE NORA
ANYMORE.

THEO YELLED AND TRIED TO HIT ME
WHEN HE FOUND OUT. I HIT HIM IN THE
FACE. NOW HE'S BLEEDING AND FATHER
IS MAD AT ME.

KING TOBIAS - AGE 9

DEAR PAPER,

THEO DOESN'T LIKE TO PLAY ANYMORE.
HE HIDES AND CLIMBS THE WALLS LIKE A
MONKEY.
I HATE HIM.

FATHER STARTED GIVING ME LESSONS. I
DON'T LIKE THESE LESSONS.

THEY HURT..

KING TOBIAS — AGE 10

DEAR PAPER,

SHE CAME TODAY. SHE WAS WITH HER

FATHER. THEO DOESN'T KNOW AND SHE

WAS GONE BEFORE HE SAW.

SHE DOESN'T REMEMBER ME.

SHE ACTED LIKE WE NEVER MET.

SHE WAS QUIET. AND SHE LOOKED REAL

PRETTY IN HER RED DRESS.

SHE LOOKED SO SAD.

WHY ARE YOU SAD ELA?

KING TOBIAS – AGE 10

DEAR PAPER,

I PASSED MY TRAINING TODAY.
SWORDSMEN LINK SAID THAT I AM BETTER
THAN ALL OF THE OTHER GUARDS.

OF COURSE I AM!

I'M THE KING.

KING TOBIAS - AGE 11

Hello,

I met a girl today. Her name is Nylah and her

parents work on the grounds. She's from Tatus and

has the reddest hair. It looks like fire.

King Tobias - Age 13

Hello,

Nylah kissed me and I ran. Who does she think she is? Kissing a king?

She's going to get herself beheaded.

King Tobias - Age 13

HELLO,

THEO SAYS HE HAS A GIRLFRIEND. HER NAME IS DALIA. SHE

LIKES FLOWERS SO I PICKED ALL OF THEM THAT I COULD

FIND AND GAVE THEM TO HER.

SHE'S MY GIRLFRIEND NOW.

KING TOBIAS - AGE 14

HELLO,

ELAENOR IS 12 NOW. FATHER SAYS WE STILL CAN'T SEE
HER, BUT HE TALKS ABOUT HER A LOT.

HE VISITS HER ONCE A YEAR. HE SAYS SHE'S REALLY PRETTY
AND THAT SHE LOOKS LIKE AUNT SYBIL.

I DOUBT SHE'S AS PRETTY AS DALIA.

KING TOBIAS - AGE 14

Hello,

Theo found out I had sex with Dalia. He said that we were too young. I'm older than him.

He is too young.

Dalia had to leave though. Her parents took her out of the palace and away somewhere.

I wonder if she is sick.

KING TOBIAS - AGE 14

Hello,

I saw Nylah again. She was with one of the guard's sons, Laris I think.

He's older than all of us by a few years. He's already an adult and starting to train. I saw her kiss him.

That will be the last time she does that.

King Tobias - Age 15

I sat in the council meeting with father today. He said Labisa is unsteady and that we have to be careful. I don't know why he doesn't just crush them now. We are the strongest nation.

Who could beat us?

King Tobias - age 17

I have grown bored of Nylah and sent her away. She was fun for awhile, but she said she loved me. She can't love me. Doesn't she know I am engaged to be married? She said she doesn't care about Ela, and that she will be the royal mistress when I am King.

I don't think I'll need her after I wed.

King Tobias - age 17

Today I have turned 18. I am officially an adult and ready to be wed. I asked father if that would be soon, but he said that Ela has to be 18 as well. Which means I have to wait two years before I can marry her.

I have been having these...urges. And the kitchenmaids are all willing to indulge me. No one questions when they return with bruises and cuts. It seems word of my desires have spread. But no one can say no to me.

I wonder when Nylah is coming back?

King Tobias - age 18

Pakin has entertained my...<u>interest</u> in herbs such as poppy and hemlock. He thinks I have an interest in botany, and I am letting him think as-such.

He agreed to source some for me so I can conduct tests. Father seems to approve of my scientific endeavours, but he doesn't really know the truth behind them.

I have two years to perfect it.

Two years until she's here.

King Tobias - age 18

A small shipment arrived today from Zivell. Inside contained vials of at least ten herbs and plants. There are only two I care about, but I had to act as if my interest was in more than toxins.

I have set up a small desk in the infirmary, in which Apollo has not questioned. He seems even more thrilled.

He's watching me and on some level, I think he knows what I am doing.

King Tobias - age 18

She died. I don't remember her name, but it seems that the combination of

poppy and hemlock was off. She took a few sips of the wine and started

gasping for breath.

I don't know why the sight of it just made me excited.

Made me HUNGRY.

King Tobias - age 18

The shadows have always been there. Lurking under my skin. Mother warned me about them when I was a child. I always hid from them, but something is happening.

They are growing stronger and I can see them.

I can <u>control them.</u>

King Tobias - age 18

I am changing dosages and testing as many women who are willing. As willing as they can be if they don't actually know what I am doing.

I had some success last night. Only 60 cc's for her estimated 54 kgs. She was loose, fun, and when the first blade sliced through her skin and she started screaming, I felt this rush of...euphoria at the sight.
When she awoke, she had no recollection. I deposited her outside, and no one knows I had anything to do with it.

This might actually work.

King Tobias - age 18

I ran tests today. And when she started bleeding, I felt the shadows surge.

I placed my hand on her stomach and the blood dissipated. Her skin closed

and I watched as I healed her.

This is how I will get away with it.

King Tobias - age 18

One year.

I have one year to reach perfection.

King Tobias - age 18

I have become quite good at controlling the shadows. I can enter the heads

of guards, make them see things that aren't there. But one person-who has

my full attention, is father.

His mind is invigorating to play in.

King Tobias - age 18

Father is getting sick. Apollo says it is a sickness of the mind.

He's right.

Father is getting sick. Apollo says it is a sickness of the mind.

King Tobias - age 19

Theo has returned from the border. He's been stationed there the last couple of years. As the second son, his only role is to serve me.

Captain of the Guard is the highest he will ever be.

He looks different. He no longer looks like a little boy.

King Tobias - age 19

I intercepted a raven today. It seems my future bride is somewhat of a hassle. Her father remarks on her ability to hide, one she's had since she was a child. She escapes into the woods and runs for hours at a time. He told us of his methods of discipline.

I have to say...

I approve.

King Tobias - age 19

Father seems to forget the time. He thinks he's a teenager again. He thinks I am his brother, the one who died during their childhood.

Oh no. Whatever will Noterra do to help their sickened King?

Rise.

King Tobias - age 19

The council has approached me.

They are ready for me to step up.

So am I.

The council has approached me.

King Tobias - age 19

I am 20 today.

Elaenor will be 18 in a couple weeks. I am ready for her.

The poppy and hemlock are ready.

My outfitted chambers are ready.

She just has to arrive.

King Tobias - age 20

Father barely leaves his chambers and when he does, he goes on and on about how Sybil will be joining us soon.

Good.

The more confused and distracted he is, the easier this will be. He's been getting nose bleeds. I think I have been playing in his mind too much, but that only makes this easier.

He won't have to be usurped if he's dead.

King Tobias - age 20

I sent a raven and called for Elaenor to arrive early. I used my father's seal, the seal that will be mine any day now.

She just has to arrive.

King Tobias - age 20

She never arrived.

A search party has been deployed. One Theo demanded he control. Fine. I don't mind. Whatever finds her quickest.

She can't slip through my fingers that soon.

I have need of her.

King Tobias - age 20

She is not what I expected. Underneath the blood and dirt and my brother's

cloak, she is beautiful. Pale skin, inky hair. I hate to admit my breath

caught when I laid eyes upon her. She is unconscious in the infirmary. Stab

wounds, scrapes, and bruises upon bruises litter her body.

Apollo confirmed my worst fears.

My Ela was raped.

King Tobias - age 20

She still has not awoken and the urge to try and heal her is strong, but it would raise too many questions. Apollo is keeping an eye on her, and I spend as much time by her side as possible. A flush has returned to her cheeks and every breath bathes me in the scent of vanilla. I can't stay away from her.

The bruises are fading and that pleases me. The only person who can mark her is me.

And mark her I will.

King Tobias - age 20

Theo is obsessed with her. Just like he was as a child. I catch him sitting

with her when I have meetings. He loves her. I can see it.

It makes me sick.

King Tobias - age 20

She has awoken today. As I write this, she is currently in the bath. Her wounds are still present, but I can take care of her. I can be her gentle knight, the one who shows her tenderness and love. And then, after we are wed, things will change.

I will have her in all ways.

King Tobias - age 20

Her lips taste like honey. Her body warm and soft.

That was until she bled all over me. And then Theo was her white knight.

I think I might kill him.

She is fine, thank gods. And I am happy to report that she is not pregnant

with that monster's child. She is ready for me.

King Tobias - age 20

My father attacked her. I may have gone too far.

He thought she was Sybil and tried to rape her. I don't know how she got away, but she did. I think it's time to end it. For good. She's in danger.

King Tobias - age 20

Something is wrong with Elaenor.

She awoke last night and stared at me in horror before racing out of the

room screaming. She looked terrified. Does she know?

She threw herself off the balcony and I almost thought that was it, but then

she kept running. She got on her horse and took off.

It took hours for us to catch up to her and when we did, she was being

attacked by savages. I had too much fun slicing their heads off.

But once again, it was Theo who she saw rescue her. He was her white

knight.

King Tobias - age 20

She is finally 18. We will be wed tomorrow. She is currently asleep in

the bed, pleased and sated after a delightful morning in the bath together.

She seems to be fairly open with her body. I can tell in her eyes she is

falling for me.

Good.

Tomorrow is the day.

King Tobias - age 20

He is dead. My father is dead.

Finally.

But a moment I have been waiting for is ruined.

Theo kissed her. He pledged his love and asked her to run away with him. She said no, thank the gods, but her lips touched his. And when my fist continuously met his face and she tried to stop me...

I hit her.

Fuck.

She forgives me.

I am King.

She is my wife.

And I have been inside of her.

All is well.

She forgives me.

King Tobias - age 20

Her face is so soft. I can't stop touching her.

But I had to leave her in bed. Nylah has called for me.

King Tobias - age 20

She is pregnant.

Nylah is pregnant.

Laris is figuring out the best way to get Nylah out of the palace. I won't let

her ruin what I have with Elaenor. I won't let her.

King Tobias - age 20

Theo is gone.

Elaenor is now the Queen. She thinks Jeremiah is her attacker in the woods, but does it really matter? He can't do anything now.

I lost my temper and hit her, and then I raped her.

It's time I start using the drugs. She can't remember me like this. She has to love me.

King Tobias - age 20

Dose 1: Taken with food, no effect. 35cc's used on 55kg.

Dose 2: Taken with other liquids to dilute taste, no effects. 35cc's used on

55kg.

Dose 1: Taken with food, no effect. 35cc's used on 55kg.

King Tobias - age 20

Dose 3: 40cc's used on 55kg. Slight drowsiness.

Dose 4: 40cc's used on 55kg. Added to wine in one dose instead of

spreading it out. Drowsiness.

King Tobias - age 20

It has been ten days and she refuses to look at me.

I invited her to the council meeting today. I just need her attention. She'll

have no excuse but to talk to me in there.

King Tobias - age 20

We fought.

Good.

It is better than the silence.

King Tobias - age 20

Dose 17: Dosages have steadily increased, utilizing liquids to mask the taste.

Desired effect achieved, will continue usage as needed. Current 60cc on

55kg used multiple times a day.

Perfect Dose: 180cc's daily; extra 60cc's prior to action.

King Tobias - age 20

Jeremiah tried to kill her. He drugged her. He drugged MY wife. And then strangled her.

I was wrong. I thought he wouldn't touch her.

I was wrong and she blames me.

She should.

I will have fun torturing him.

King Tobias - age 20

Her present is due any day now.

King Tobias - age 20

Her wine cart is empty and she lay on the bed. Her eyes droopy as she

looks at me. I can still smell her blood and hear her screams as I finally

took out all the anger I had. All the times she defied me. All the times

Theo looked at her.

She is mine. And she won't remember any of this.

King Tobias - age 20

Her father arrived, Scarlett and Theo in tow. I planned this, but it was still a shock to see him propose to her in the middle of the festivities. And when I looked around, Elaenor was gone. She hid. Like she always does.

So I found her and had some fun. The blood soaked into her hair was a problem, so I bathed her. Dressed her in her finest silk, like my queen deserves, and laid her back to bed.

King Tobias - age 20

I lost control today. She hadn't had enough wine.

She was aware of what I was doing.

But she wasn't scared...

She smiled.

King Tobias - age 20

She knows something.

She just left the council room, a defiant look in her eyes.

I don't trust her.

King Tobias - age 20

It wasn't supposed to be this way.

Rhea is dead, one of her old ladies. And now Scarlett is fighting for her

life in the infirmary.

She can't die. Ela will never forgive me.

But he told her. Theo told her about the drugs. How does he know? He

has to die, but for now, he's chained to a stone slab.

King Tobias - age 20

Apollo is aware of what I have been doing.

He doesn't care, that sick bastard. He's preparing syringes for me. Regularly injecting her so she stays unaware of time.

I am having a lot of fun with her now. All times of the day.

She's mine.

King Tobias - age 20

Scarlett is missing.

FUCK

Scarlett is missing.

She was lucid today.

I have to up the dose.

On the other hand, the army has started the trek to Chatis.

It should be gone by tomorrow.

King Tobias - age 20

It was him. Of course it was.

And I had to slice my own brother's head off in front of my wife. He was trying to take her.

AGAIN.

I wish I could kill him all over again. She's asleep in the bed, soaked in his blood.

Good.

She'll see more blood tomorrow.

King Tobias - age 20

I pulled her through the ruined streets. Let her feet bleed and her legs grow cold.

She has to know what lengths I would go to in order to keep her.

She has no home to return to. No friends or family.

She only has me.

King Tobias - age 20

Bladesmiths and welders have been at my beck and call lately.

I can't believe how many new instruments I have.

I can't believe how good it feels to use them on her.

King Tobias - age 20

Thelonious is here. I don't know how it's possible. But if I can use him to gain access to another country...I'll do it.

But Ela, she's a problem. He is her uncle, he will worry about her. She has to see him, show him that she is okay.

She has to believe it.

King Tobias - age 20

I was gone for an hour after having an incredible night with my wife. She was...warm and loving. She slept in my arms as if it were the summer again.

And then - fucking Davel touched what's mine. And what's even worse, is this wasn't the first time. I'm going to kill him, but I am going to do it slowly and I am going to figure out how many men have been between her legs.

And kill them too.

King Tobias - age 20

I left again - for only hours. And this woman, this fucking wife of mine thought it would be fine to NOT show the world who she is.   -

She took it off. She took her fucking crown off.

She'll never do that again. I will make sure of it.

King Tobias - age 20

Nylah has returned. She brought with her a son.

MY SON.

Nylah has returned. She brought with her a son.

King Tobias - age 20

She can't be allowed to exist. This is my heir. And he will be raised by my wife.

This is our child now.

King Tobias - age 20

Ela has taken to Cynfael like a good little wife.

She is caring for him, she is loving him.

And I don't have to lift a finger. I go to her when I need her, no drugs

needed any more. Heal her with the shadows, and go about my day.

Life is perfect.

King Tobias - age 20

He's gone.

The one thing I fucking asked her for and she ruined it. How am I supposed to rule without an heir?

This whore. This piece of trash was never meant to be queen. She deserves everything that's going to happen to her down there.

All of it.

I can hear her screams, her whimpers as men touch her.

Rape her.

I should feel bad. But I don't.

She is just a stupid human girl, and I am a God.

A KING.

King Tobias - age 21

Magic. How is that possible? The blinding white light, the feel of the

streams of magic burning through my skin. She actually wounded me. And

then, her hair. It turned this brilliant shade of white. My gods she was

beautiful. My wife is a god also. She's perfect in every way.

And they took her. Labisa took her from me. I will get her back. I have to

get her back.

My little goddess needs to come home to me.

My perfect little Ela.

King Tobias - age 21

She's scared. I saw her face as that piece of shit man pulled her off a cliff.

He could have killed my Ela. He could have KILLED her.

I will destroy him. But I can't enter Rakushia now.

I need help.

King Tobias - age 21

Nero is there. Gods what an easy job it was to infiltrate their ranks. He's

there and he is going to get close to her.

He will protect her.

King Tobias - age 21

She thinks she's married.

MARRIED??

To the Prince of Labisa.

No. That's not true. She already belongs to me.

She's mine.

She doesn't love him. They don't even speak.

This is good.

She misses me.

I should visit her. I need to see my wife.

King Tobias - age 21

My Ela is coming home to me. She asked Nero for help. She's coming home. My little goddess will resume her place beside me.

I miss her. Gods I miss her.

I will never let her go again.

King Tobias - age 21

No.

No.

NO.

NO.

No.

No.

this isn't real

I killed her.

It was an accident, a reflex. I killed her. She was pregnant. She said she

was pregnant. My wife is dead. And I killed her.

King Tobias - age 21

Her body stays warm, stays clean.

I won't allow this to be real.

I will figure out how to bring her back. I will. For now, I will rest beside my little goddess.

Beside My Ela.

King Tobias - age 21

Book Series

<u>The Diadem</u>

Glass and Bone

Cages and Crowns

<u>The Diadem Short Stories</u>

Elaenor

Tobias

Author Note

This journal series started as a passion project and ended up as a way to bridge the gap between book one and two. And now, we have journal number two to bridge the gap between book 2 and 4. (Yes book 4 because book 3 is a prequel...spoiler!)

This journal contains spoilers for Glass and Bone as well as Cages and Crowns. With that being said, it can be read at any time.

Who should I do next?

XO Celaena

About the Author

Celaena Cuico (sell-ay-nuh coo-we-co) is a 28 year old bisexual that was born and raised in Southern California. She was raised with two parents and an older sister, as well as an army of pets. Celaena endured hardships such as an abusive significant other-and the unknown that comes with moving across the country twice for a job. She is the author of The Diadem, a series about a young girl thrown into a life of jumping from kingdom to kingdom to survive, as well as the author of a new series called The Soulless, which follows servants of Lucifer.

www.ingramcontent.com/pod-product-compliance
Lightning Source LLC
Chambersburg PA
CBHW070422310726
48977CB00003B/804